Dooby
Dooby
moo

For Mom
–D. C.

To Claire Rose Reilly
and Logan Patrick McMurray
–B. L.

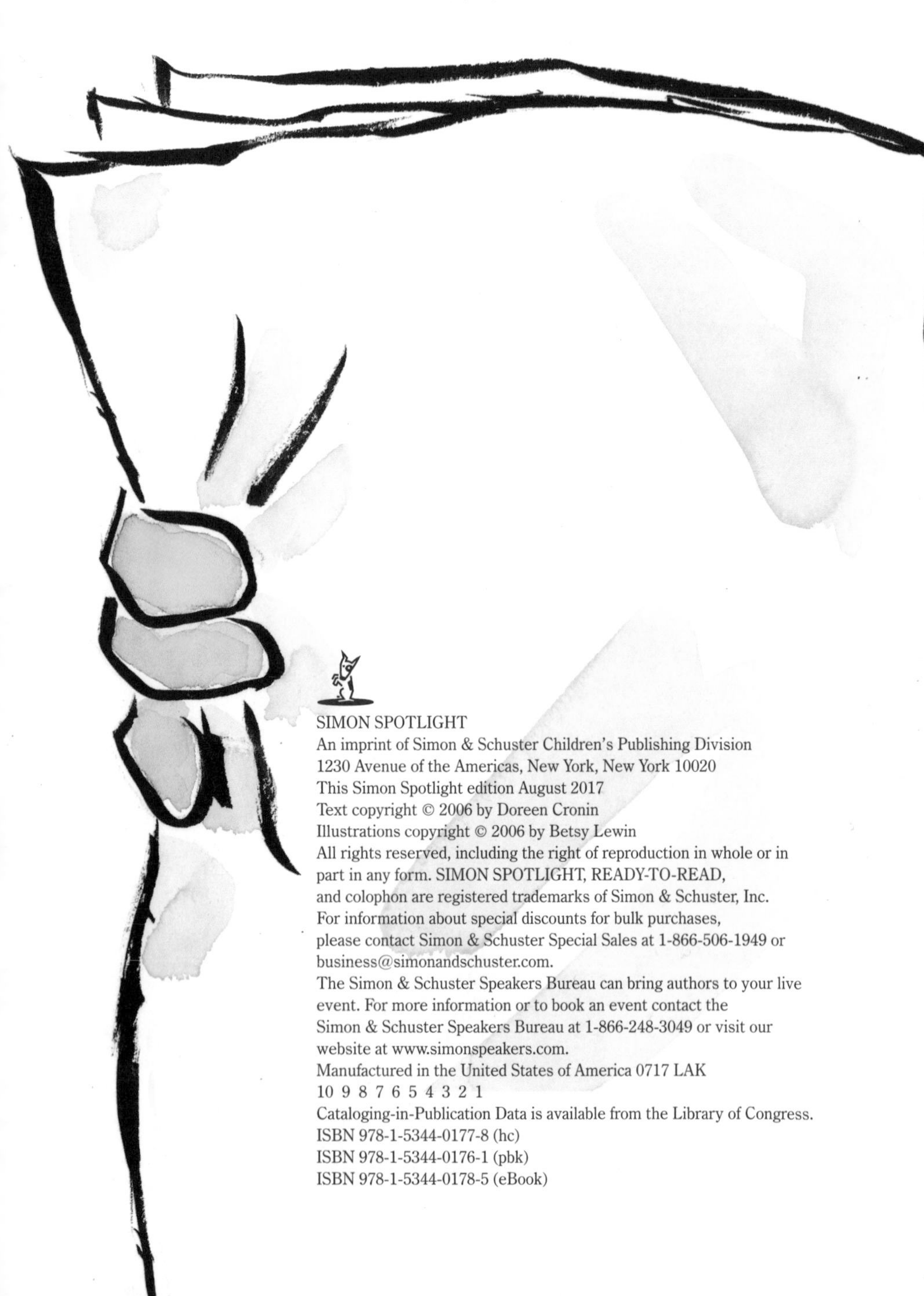

SIMON SPOTLIGHT
An imprint of Simon & Schuster Children's Publishing Division
1230 Avenue of the Americas, New York, New York 10020
This Simon Spotlight edition August 2017

Manufactured in the United States of America 0717 LAK
10 9 8 7 6 5 4 3 2 1
Cataloging-in-Publication Data is available from the Library of Congress.
ISBN 978-1-5344-0177-8 (hc)
ISBN 978-1-5344-0176-1 (pbk)
ISBN 978-1-5344-0178-5 (eBook)

by
doreen cronin
and
betsy lewin

Ready-to-Read

Simon Spotlight
New York London Toronto Sydney New Delhi

Farmer Brown keeps a very close eye
on his animals.
Every night he listens
outside the barn door.

Dooby, dooby moo . . .
the cows snore.

Fa la, la, la baaaa . . .
the sheep snore.

Whacka, whacka quack . . .
Duck snores.

Duck keeps a very close eye
on Farmer Brown.
Every morning Duck borrows
his newspaper. One day,
an ad catches his eye:

TALENT SHOW!!!

OPEN TO ALL!!

where: **COUNTY FAIR**
when: **SATURDAY**

1st prize: **A TRAMPOLINE!!**

2nd prize: **BOX OF CHALK**

3rd prize: **VEGGIE CHOP-O-MATIC**

WELCOME
DAILY POST

As soon as Farmer Brown opened his paper, he knew the animals were up to something.

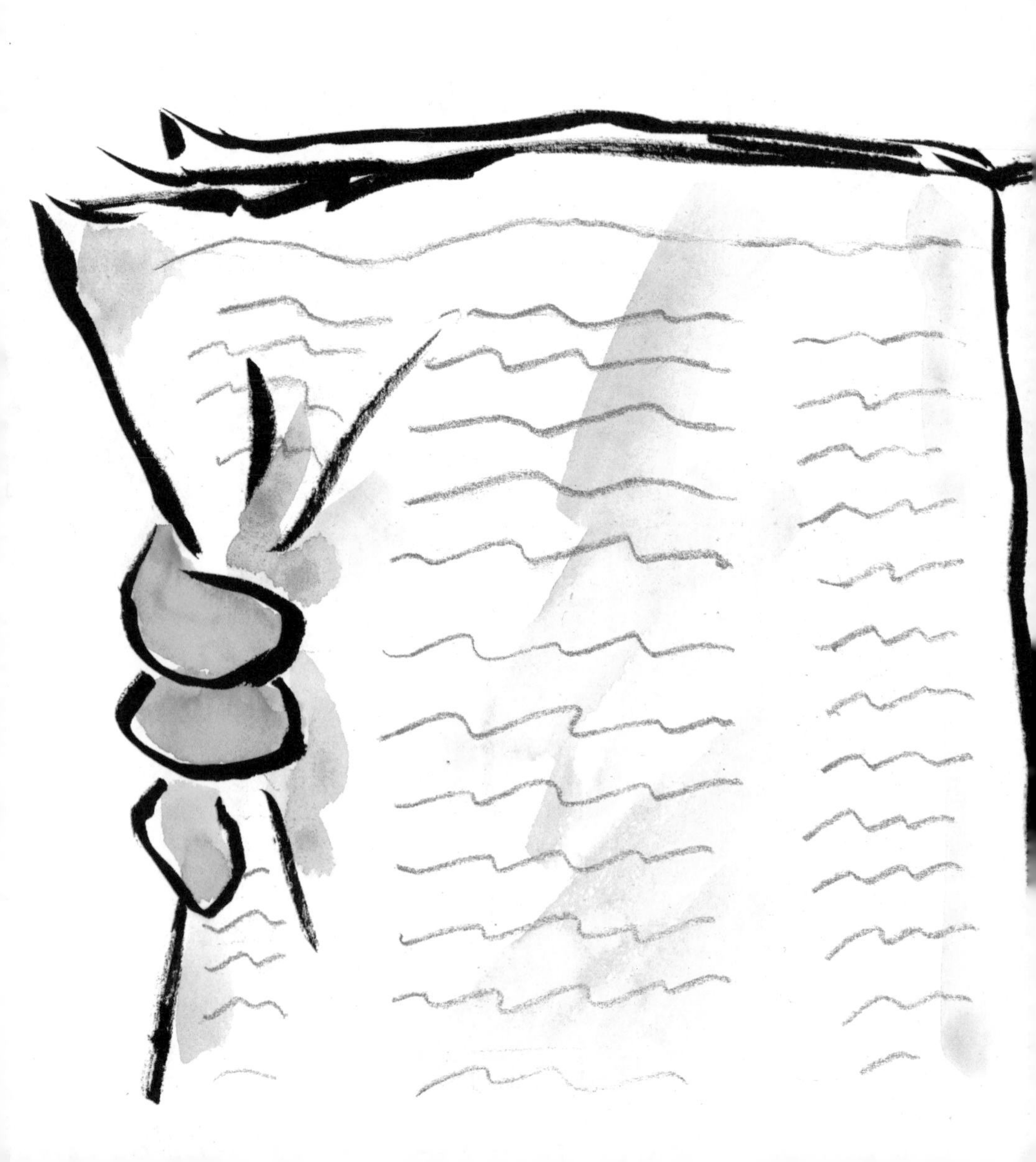

DAILY POST

Farmer Brown watched them closely all day. He watched them from above.

He watched them from below.

He even watched them upside down.

Outside the barn, late at night,
he heard,

Dooby, dooby moo . . .
Fa la, la, la baaaa . . .
Whacka, whacka quack . . .

Inside the barn, the cows rehearsed "Twinkle, Twinkle, Little Star."

Dooby, dooby, dooby moo.
Dooby moo, moo, moo, moo, moo.

Needs work, Duck noted.

The sheep rehearsed
"Home on the Range."

Baaa, baaa, baaa, baaabaaa.

Fa la baaa, fa la baaaa,
baaaabaaabaaa!

Duck had them try it again,
with more feeling.

The pigs did an interpretive dance.

snored Duck.

Day after day, Farmer Brown kept a very close eye on the animals.

He watched from the left.

He watched from the right.

He even watched in disguise.

Outside the barn, night after night,
he heard:

Dooby, dooby moo . . .

Fa la, la, la baaaa . . .

Whacka, whacka quack . . .

Inside the barn, night after night,
the animals rehearsed.

Finally it was time
for the county fair.
Duck was pacing back and forth.

The pigs were combing their hair.

The cows were drinking tea with lemon.

They ARE up to something! thought Farmer Brown. Farmer Brown was not going to leave them alone.

He loaded all the animals
into the back of his truck
and drove to the fair.

When he got there he heard:

He parked his truck and headed off to the free barbecue.

When Farmer Brown was out of sight,
the animals ran
to the talent show desk
and signed in.

The cows sang
"Twinkle, Twinkle, Little Star."

Dooby, dooby, dooby moo.
Dooby moo, moo, moo, moo, moo.

Two of the judges were
clearly impressed.

The sheep sang
"Home on the Range."

Fa la, la, la baa.

Fa la baaa,

ba, ba, baaa, baa, ba, baaaa.

Three of the judges were
clearly impressed.

It was time for the pigs' interpretive dance.
But they were sound asleep.

Shloink oink, oink, oink, oink.

All of the judges were clearly annoyed.

Duck really wanted that trampoline.
He jumped on stage and sang
"Born to Be Wild."*

QUACK, QUACK, QUACK,
QUUUAAAAAACKK!

The judges gave him
a standing ovation.

* Original words and music by Mars Bonfire

When Farmer Brown got back
to the truck, he heard:

Dooby, dooby moo . . .
Fa la, la, la baaaa . . .
Whacka, whacka quack . . .

The animals were exactly where
he had left them.

FAIRGROUNDS

That night Farmer Brown listened outside the barn door.

Dooby, dooby BOING!

Fa la, la, la BOING!

Whacka, whacka BOING!